Special thanks:
Andi Triyanta
Stacy Zieger

A Tribute:

Thank you, Alexus, for choosing me.
You continue to change the world without knowing or trying.
Whether you see the world through the walls of your room or in a hospital room, I
will always make sure the world knows you.
Here's to you and all of the kids we hope to inspire.
You have always believed in me, but this is your faith at work.

A note from

The Author

This story is a small piece of change in physical form.
As my bright eyes gazed into the lights of my best friend's
hospital room, I dreamt of a world that embraced differences.
You are reading that dream.

If we all create small pieces of change, we will begin to evolve the
future of humankind.

Chase your dreams wildly. Believe in your uniqueness.
Dare to take a chance.

Thank you for supporting a purpose that began before I was
born. And thank you to all who see the importance of this work.

This is just the beginning.
James 2:26

Savvy Sammi

by Trinity Jagdeo

"Hey, Mom, did you know that axolotls can regenerate their body parts?" Sammi asked. "Did you also know that–"

"That's great, Sammi! How about you save some of your fun facts for the aquarium today? Let's finish up your schoolwork before we go." Sammi's mom stated.

"Eek! I love amphibians and all types of animals. I can't wait for the new exhibit, Zeek!" Sammi said.

"We're just in time!" Sammi smiled.

"Come one, come all! Today is the day we will reveal our brand new axolotl exhibit! As part of the reveal, we'll share some facts about this critically endangered species," the marine biologist announced. As Sammi listened to the marine biologist, a mysterious man made his way through the crowd. "Ahem! Oh," the man murmured to Sammi. "My sincerest apologies for bumping into you; we're just trying to make our way...out. Pardon us."

The marine biologist continued, "And, axolotls are carnivores. How fact-tastic! Without further ado, we present to you the incredible axolotl exhibit!"

Suddenly, the crowd gasped, and the marine biologist shrieked in disbelief. "Oh, my octopus! The axolotls are… missing!"

As the crowd stood shocked, Sammi wondered if the thief could be seen on the security cameras. She quietly left the exhibit to find the security room. When she found it, she noticed something on one of the surveillance screens.

On the screen, she saw the mysterious man from the exhibit room morph into a sea creature and everyone trapped in an unknown substance!

"I have to do something about this," Sammi exclaimed. "The axolotls are missing, and the visitors are in danger. We have to rescue them!"

"Zeek, come out from hiding in my backpack. I knew I would need you for a reason. It's time to activate... Savvy Sammi!"

"Let's check the showcase arena first, and then the -" Sammi was interrupted.

"Stop right there, missy!" someone yelled. "Who are you?" Sammi asked.

"I'm Jilly the Jellyfish. Don't remember me? The tall man, known as the infamous Scorpio the Squidnapper, and I bumped into you earlier. I'm the Squidnapper's fabulous assistant, or as I call myself, the greatest villain yet to come. Somehow, you managed to slip away from everyone, so you'll get to see our villain skills at work! After we snatch these rare sea animals, we will auction them for money! We'll be filthy rich! Though, of course, I can never remember the names of these critters. I think one was a starfish, a beluga whale, or a sea clam. Oh, I know it's a - "

As Jilly rattled to herself, she forgot Sammi was there. Sammi quickly tried to remember animal facts she learned from her schoolwork to stop Jilly.

"Think! Think! Think!" Sammi thought to herself. That's it! I remember that jellyfish are made up of eighty percent water. Zeek, let's turn the heat up!" Sammi shouted.

Zeek rushed to the thermostat as Jilly rambled, "Or maybe, a dolphin? Oh no, no. Maybe a hammerhead shark? I think that's it." The temperature in the room began to rise.

"Oh, man. I'm not feeling so well. I can't... feel my... tentacles," Jilly groaned as she collapsed from the heat.

As Jilly lay still, Sammi thought about the next steps. "We can't leave her here, Zeek," she realized. "We have to keep Jilly contained while we search for Scorpio."

Sammi thought of an idea. "Ah, I know. Let's tie her up with bandages! My mom's specialty is wrapping my injuries, so I know a thing or two about keeping things still." Sammi and Zeek wrapped Jilly with bandages. "And…done!" Sammi huffed.

"High four, Zeek, great teamwork," she exclaimed. "Now, let's track down Scorpio before he harms more marine life. I heard Jilly mention starfish; let's find that exhibit."

While Jilly stayed wrapped up, Sammi set out to find Scorpio.

While Sammi looked for the starfish exhibit, she suddenly felt a weird vibration.

"Let's check that noise out! The sound is coming from this way," Sammi pointed. "Oh, but it's not wheelchair accessible. I'll need to use my teleportation superpower!"

"Without my superpower, I would miss out on this exhibit because I can't use the stairs, so let's teleport!"

"Zeek, look over there, we're too late. Shards of glass and water are everywhere," Sammi whispered. "Gah! Scorpio hypnotized those crabs to be his henchmen. It seems like he never planned on using his sidekick Jilly after all. He's doing this all on his own."

Sammi continued, "He's already relocating the starfish, so we must find the next sea creature he planned to steal before he gets away. Jilly mentioned a sea clam, but I don't see any here." Sammi wondered, "Hmm…maybe she meant the rare oyster exhibit!"

"We have no time to waste, let's go find out!" Sammi rushed off.

As Scorpio continued with his evil plan, Sammi raced to the oyster exhibit and found the rare oyster, Ortencia, safe and sound.

"Here she is! Let's warn her. Animal communication, commence!" Sammi used her animal telepathy superpower to talk to Ortencia. "Ms. Ortencia Osyter, you're in danger!" Sammi explained. "An evil squid named Scorpio is planning to steal you and your pearls! We have to trap him before he harms more sea animals!"

Together, they conspired on a plan to defeat Scorpio.

"Well, Savvy Sammi, if that irritant squid comes to steal my pearls, we will trick him! We'll replace my real pearl with a fake, poisonous one. Squids are resilient, so this will only keep him dazed, but it will give you time to save more friends," Ortencia planned.

Before Scorpio arrived, Ortencia made a fake pearl while Sammi watched from afar.

"My, what a pretty creature! You would make an excellent dinner, and your precious pearls will make me rich!" Scorpio smirked. "Don't mind me; I'm just going to take this-"

Suddenly, Scorpio eeked.

"Ah!" he shouted. He quickly became ill and fell to the ground after touching the fake pearl.

After the evil squid fell, Sammi raced to the next exhibit that Jilly mentioned - the beluga whale exhibit.

"Hey, baby beluga whale! What's your name? You're in danger, and we must find a way out of this tank. Do you have a way to get out?" Sammi asked.

"Oh, no! My name is AJ, and there's no way out. Well, there might be one way, but I'm too afraid to try!" the baby whale sighed.

"Why be fearful when you can be brave? Scorpio will take you if you don't get out of there now! I'll be right here to encourage you along the way. We can do this!" Sammi encouraged.

"Well, there's space behind this tank wall that I can hide behind. It's a resting space when we don't have aquarium visitors," AJ explained. "Usually, there's an easy pathway to get there, but the crew locked it before they disappeared. Now, I can only get there if I leap over this wall, but I'm not sure if I can make it," AJ worried.

"I understand how you feel, AJ, but we can only become stronger when we push ourselves! I believe in you, and so does Zeek. All you have to do is try! If you don't make it, we'll figure out a different plan," Sammi said confidently.

Sammi placed her hand on the tank so AJ could feel her supernatural encouraging power. Shortly after, AJ swam swiftly over the tank wall and into the resting space for hiding.

"I did it! I did it! I can't believe it!" AJ splashed around with glee.

"I knew you could, AJ! Now hang tight while I take out this villain once and for all!" Sammi said with pride.

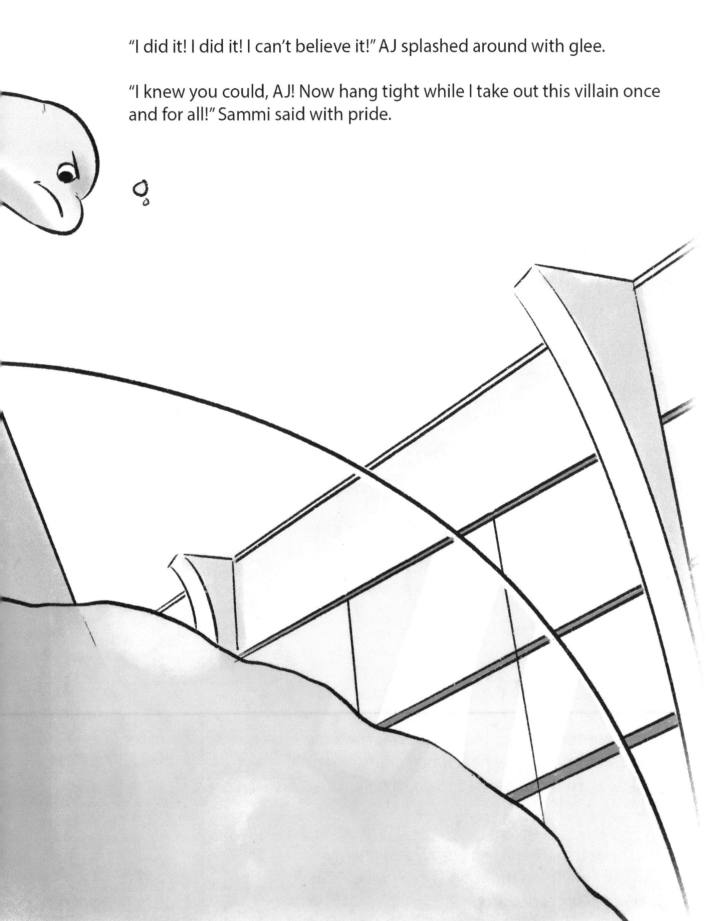

As Sammi raced back to the oyster exhibit to find Scorpio, she spotted his henchmen huddled around the outdoor exhibits. Scorpio was back on his tentacles directing the henchmen crabs! Sammi knew what she needed to do to defeat Scorpio.

"We will have to gather a squid's biggest enemy - albatrosses! One thing those birds can't resist is a tasty squid!" Sammi declared.

Sammi zipped to the albatross enclosure and spoke to them. With Zeek's help, they unlocked the bird cage and directed them to Scorpio and his henchmen.

"Stop right there. It's over for you, Scorpio! You've taken enough sea mammals and destroyed too many exhibits. You're busted!" Sammi yelled. Then, the flock squawked at Scorpio and carried him away.

As Scorpio was carried away, his spell wore off; the henchman crabs, aquarium staff, and visitors were freed.

While things were restored at the aquarium, Sammi thought about the stolen creatures. "I'm worried about the starfish and the other sea creatures Scorpio stole. How will we ever get them back?" Sammi sighed.

Unexpectedly, Sammi heard the sound of tires squealing. She turned around and discovered Jilly was behind her.

"Did you think you could get rid of me that easily?" Jilly said with a smile. "After recovering from that heat exhaustion, I saw Scorpio's plan to leave without me. I couldn't believe he was going to ditch me! So, I decided to help defeat his ultimate plan and do the right thing. I found his getaway truck with all the stolen sea creatures inside!" Jilly pointed. "And, now I can help the aquarium crew put them back where they belong," she added.

Sammi gleamed with pride. "Thank you, Jilly! It looks like you didn't need to be a villain to be one of the greatest. With your help, these animals are safe and out of harm's way!"

Moments later ...

An hour after the aquarium came back to life, Sammi, her family, and her new friend Jilly walked and rolled around the new exhibits. Sammi began to read, "See, here it says axolotls can regenerate their heart, lungs, and brain-"

"Look, Sammi! Over there!" Jilly interrupted.

An aquarium staff member, Victoria, noticed the crowd around a new enclosure and walked over to introduce the sea animal.

"Oh! This guy?" Victoria began, "He's our newest addition! We were told he could be dangerous, so we placed him in a protective enclosure. Our aquarium staff found him at the entrance doors, squished into a little glass jar! We heard rumors that some girl in a cape had something to do with it! My - it has been a crazy day!" Victoria laughed with confusion.

"It was a crazy day, but nothing that Savvy Sammi couldn't handle!" Sammi thought to herself.

The End.

 *Proverbs 82:4*

Rescue the weak and the needy;
deliver them from the hand of the wicked.

Character inspired by:

Sammi Haney

Emmy nominated actress

> I'm so glad to be in a book that lets kids with disabilities see themselves. I'm also a huge animal lover, so I love being a part of this story.

About The Nonprofit:

From We Can't to We Can is a nonprofit organization that aims to raise representation statistics for the disability community. The organization's mission promotes inclusion and embraces diversity through children's books, events, and programs.

For more information (and superheroes):
www.wecant2wecan.org

Trinity Jagdeo

the author

Trinity Jagdeo is a Generation Z aspiring world changer. A
daring dreamer, Jagdeo has been described as seeing the
world for what it could be. She prides herself in wearing
multiple hats: founder, author, and motivational speaker.
Jagdeo's efforts are among many major publications like
Forbes and the Today Show. An advocate for change, her
"heart-work" has been recognized with prestigious awards,
including F4Y Humanitarian Award, New Jersey Heartland
Hero, and 30 under 30 Trendsetter.

CPSIA information can be obtained
at www.ICGtesting.com
Printed in the USA
JSHW072345010523
41121JS00002B/25